IT'S TOO TOO WINDY!

by Hans Wilhelm

Hello Reader! — Level 1

SCHOLASTIC INC.

New York Toronto London Auckland Sydney Mexico City Ne

I don't want to go outside!

Hello, Family Members,

Learning to read is one of the most important accomplishments of early childhood. **Hello Reader!** books are designed to help children become skilled readers who like to read. Beginning readers learn to read by remembering frequently used words like "the," "is," and "and"; by using phonics skills to decode new words; and by interpreting picture and text clues. These books provide both the stories children enjoy and the structure they need to read fluently and independently. Here are suggestions for helping your child *before*, *during*, and *after* reading:

Before

- Look at the cover and pictures and have your child predict what the story is about.
- Read the story to your child.
- Encourage your child to chime in with familiar words and phrases.
- Echo read with your child by reading a line first and having your child read it after you do.

During

- Have your child think about a word he or she does not recognize right away. Provide hints such as "Let's see if we know the sounds" and "Have we read other words like this one?"
- Encourage your child to use phonics skills to sound out new words.
- Provide the word for your child when more assistance is needed so that he or she does not struggle and the experience of reading with you is a positive one.
- Encourage your child to have fun by reading with a lot of expression . . . like an actor!

After

- Have your child keep lists of interesting and favorite words.
- Encourage your child to read the books over and over again. Have him or her read to brothers, sisters, grandparents, and even teddy bears. Repeated readings develop confidence in young readers.
- Talk about the stories. Ask and answer questions. Share ideas about the funniest and most interesting characters and events in the stories.

I do hope that you and your child enjoy this book.

—Francie Alexander
Reading Specialist,
Scholastic's Learning Ventures

Go to www.scholastic.com for Web site information
on Scholastic authors and illustrators.

Copyright © 2000 by Hans Wilhelm, Inc.
All rights reserved. Published by Scholastic Inc.
SCHOLASTIC, HELLO READER, CARTWHEEL BOOKS and associated logos
are trademarks and/or registered trademarks of Scholastic Inc.

Library of Congress Cataloging-in-Publication Data

Wilhelm, Hans, 1945-
    It's too windy! / by Hans Wilhelm.
        p.   cm. — (Hello reader! Level 1)
    Summary: The family dog finds a clever way to stop Baby's stroller from
rolling away.
    ISBN 0-439-10849-7
    [1. Dogs—Fiction.] I. Title. II. Series.
PZ7.W64816It   2000
[E] — dc21   99-29842
                                                                        CIP
                                                                        AC
10 9 8 7 6 5 4 3 2 1   0/0   01   02   03   04
                            Printed in the U.S.A.   24
                        First printing, February 2000

I want to stay inside.

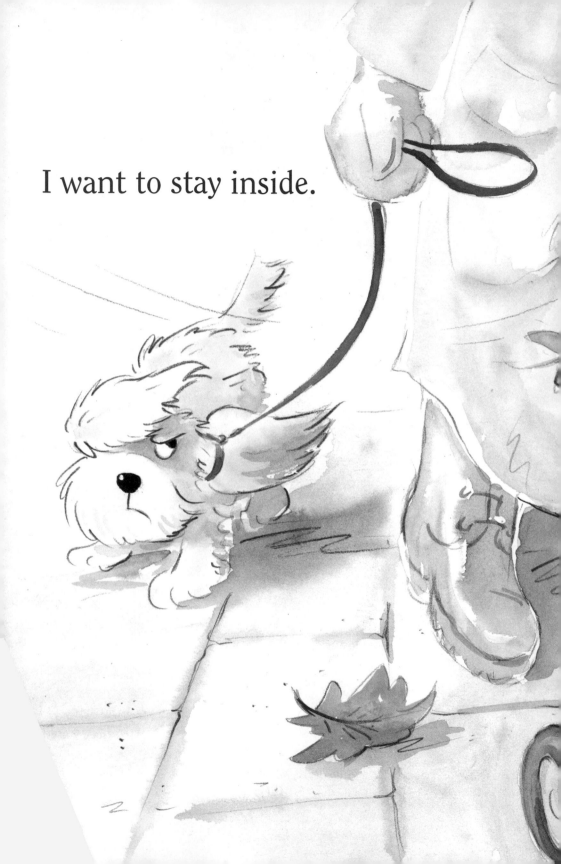

It's too windy.

I hate waiting.

The wind is pulling Baby and me.

The stroller is rolling.
I can't stop it.

Nobody sees us!

What can I do?

I see a street lamp.

I have an idea!

I know how to stop this
rolling stroller.

I did it!

I saved Baby!

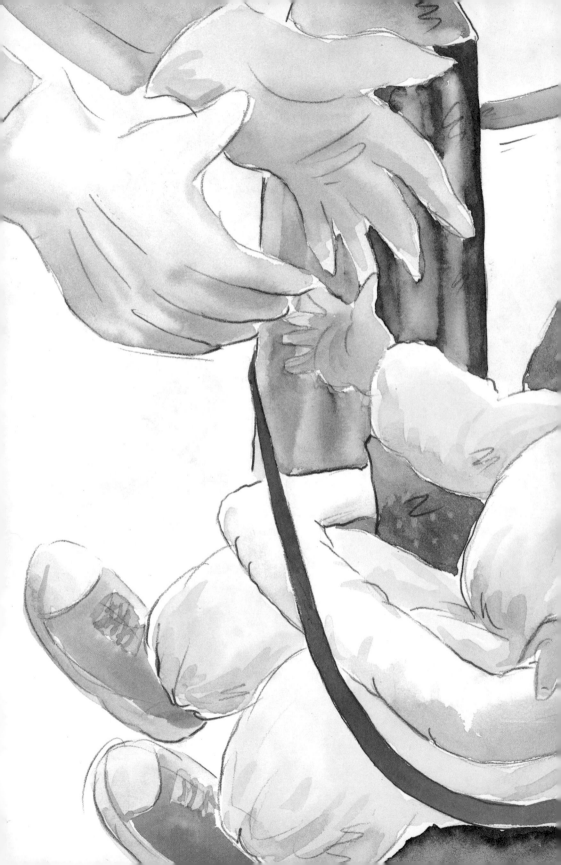

Everything is fine!

I deserve a big bone.

I got it!